The Light

Written by Teheli Sealey

Illustrated by Ros Webb

This book is dedicated in honour of all the many loving people who gave me love and light during one of the darkest periods of my life.

Special thanks to a few of these "lights";

Mark, for being there for me even when I pushed you away.

Shiron, for always giving me your time.

Natalie, for coaxing me out of my shell.

Adrian, for giving me hope and keeping a dream alive.

Khrystanne, I will always hold in my heart your sisterly love.

Love and light to you all

Thank you.

T.

Once upon a time, there was a ray of light that shined so brightly.

She shined so bright that she could brighten any dark room and make other lights shine too!

One day, this light was shining brighter than usual.

She was surrounded by other lights and the one light she loved the most.

It was a dream come true!

At the height of this special moment, this beautiful, radiant light fell from the sky and broke into pieces.

It was a very hard fall and did not seem possible that this light would ever shine again.

The other lights stood by in shock and sadness.

Yet, by some miracle, even after this very hard fall, the light was still glowing.

Though she was broken, the light had kept her spark but would need major repairs.

Repairing this light would be a long journey. She would require lots of love and of course... light!

The light felt very sad and broken.

She wondered what she had done wrong to fall from the sky in this way.

Along came the other lights.

They lifted her, picked up all her many broken pieces and placed her gently and lovingly into a cocoon.

This cocoon seemed hard on the outside, but on the inside, it was soft and extremely quiet.

Each of the other lights placed a small gift inside the cocoon to keep her company and help this once-bright light shine again.

Some placed love, some placed friendship, some placed prayer, a few thoughtful lights placed food and the rare few who knew how to touch this fragile light added **hugs**, **kisses** and **healing energy**.

When the cocoon was sealed, other lights stood outside the cocoon to protect this light from being attacked by predators.

It was dark inside the cocoon, yet the light felt comforted by the soft, warm glow she gave off.

Many times, she felt lonely and wanted to free herself from this cocoon but was too weak to do so.

The little light cried and cried.

As she wept softly to herself, the lights guarding her cocoon cried too, as they too could hear her soft cries.

As much as these lights wanted to release her from this cocoon, she had to be strong to do this for herself. The lock was on the inside you see.

It was a very sad time for all.

Sometimes, well-meaning lights would call out to her from outside the cocoon, words of encouragement or just to make sure that she was ok.

Some days she would be too weak to respond, so would knock softly on the cocoon walls to let them know she was fine, but at times would be too weak to even knock on the walls.

Some lights felt hurt thinking that she ignored them and walked away.

They didn't realize she just did not have enough strength to reply.

As time went on, the little light found the strength to glue her pieces back together.

It was very peaceful in the cocoon, but it was also **very lonely**.

There was only enough space in the cocoon for this light and her damaged pieces as she glued herself back together and to once again slowly take the shape of a light once more.

Some pieces were a lot easier to put back together than others, but there were also the tinier pieces—fragile little pieces which required special care and time to heal properly.

These fragile pieces were the most valuable parts of the light. She had to pay careful attention while gluing them back together, or they could fall apart and break into even smaller pieces than before.

One day, the light realized all her parts were glued back together and that she could move around without worry or fear of breaking into pieces once again.

She tested her strength, slowly but firmly releasing the lock on the inside of her cocoon.

As the cocoon opened up, the light was surprised! Everything around her outside looked exactly the same, yet different. As if the world she knew had lost its glow.

Around her, other lights rushed to her side to greet her with hugs and kisses, happy to see that she had left the cocoon.

But the light was afraid that she would break into pieces and would not allow herself to be touched – except by a chosen and trusted few.

Life outside the cocoon felt strange, and the light found it hard to believe that she once enjoyed shining bright and radiating light to others.

She wanted to shine again but did not know how.

Being around the other lights became hard, so she learned to dim her glow whilst walking around the other lights to avoid drawing attention to herself.

But this little light was determined to glow again; brighter and stronger.

She knew her light would never shine the same way again, and that made her sad, but she wanted to learn how she could shine again, and shine brighter!

Little by little, day by day, the little light grew brighter.

Sometimes she would get scared about breaking into pieces or falling from the sky, but she would continue to try despite her fears.

She knew she had to try!

As she burned brighter, other lights noticed and were attracted to the unique way she now radiated light.

In her presence, other lights shone brightly too, and soon she found herself surrounded by lights and sharing light with others once more.

As she shone brighter, the little light needed more space to grow and expand.

The space she radiated light with other lights became too small.

While she felt scared, she knew she had to rise again into the sky.

It was a scary time.

She didn't mind radiating light from the floor but was afraid to do it from the sky where many others could see her or she could fall.

But the little light could stay on the ground no more since she grew bigger and brighter day by day.

Gathering her courage, she took to the sky.
Shaky at first, but growing in confidence
as she radiated light.

The more she radiated, the more she grew.
So up and away, she rose.

Higher and higher she rose, far above the earth, twinkling in the night sky.

She shone her brightest at night, you see, for indeed this little light was no ordinary light but a star who had lost her way.

Now, she shines brightly far up in
the sky, touching the lives of many,
and on a really clear night, you can
see her twinkling far, far above.

About the Author

As a child, Teheli recalls being cautioned by well-meaning grownups of all the things she "could not" do but rarely what she "could" achieve if she believed.

She has been motivated ever since to inspire others to evolve their thinking - breaking free of the mental, physical and emotional limitations that she has had many personal challenges with.

Her turning point was learning to swim over 40 years old after "almost drowning" too many times. Since then moving on to become an avid athlete and open water swimmer.

The story of "The light" was inspired by Teheli's real-life traumatic experience in 2020 after sustaining a head injury when her head was run over by a car (twice). Her miraculous healing, overcoming the mental, emotional, physical, and spiritual trauma that followed in the wake of what she calls her "life-changing experience".

This book tells the age-old story of coping with trauma, PTSD, and goes full circle. From being at a high point in her life, crashing, learning to heal, love, trust again, and coming back stronger than before.

This is a beautiful and powerful message to young readers about resilience.

Teheli intends to share her story in a positive and inspiring way that will teach children and adults alike the value and power of resilience, having a strong support system, and believing in yourself.

Teheli Sealey is a certified personal trainer, health coach, Stott Pilates Instructor, Yoga Teacher, Health and Fitness Influencer, and avid athlete. She is also the founder of Get Fitspired–Join the evolution of limitless thinking and proud Mama of 4 cats!

Learn more about Teheli visit www.tehelisealey.com

Made in the USA
Middletown, DE
28 June 2022

This Book Belongs To:

A firefiter that probablee can't spell his own name

When we last left Felix, he was on top of the world. He had just became a firefighter!
He thought he would get to just run jobs all day and talk to nurses. Boy was he wrong.

For the next year Felix was yelled at as a probie
and broken down like an old mule.

He thought he was finally going to get on the guys' good side when they had him bring Chief Bear an exhaust sample from the engine.

He spent a lot of time cleaning around the station and used so much bleach all of his uniform pants got stained for the next year.

He spent the whole year answering the station phone because it's a probie's job and also because most firefighters hate talking to people on a non-emergent basis. Introverts, am I right?

Felix had to take all kinds of classes that he had to pass, even though he barely got his high school diploma.

The guys even expected him to cook dinner at the firehouse every night, even though his momma had made all his food for him everyday.

Instead of fires, he went on med calls everyday. And it seemed like every shift he was getting someone else's poop on him.

Felix started to develop an insane hatred for the police when they chose to block his fire engine from getting to a structure fire. He couldn't comprehend how they thought THEY were the heroes.

And it definitely wasn't like the movies. Any time they did have a structure fire he was always last due.

He even decided to get a tattoo that he thought the guys would LOVE. Boy was he wrong.

It also didn't take long at all for him to develop a nicotine and caffeine addiction!

And needless to say, that first big boy check went to his head. He got himself a big diesel truck he could not afford!

It also wasn't uncommon for him to get interrupted during lunch time for a med call!

And he discovered it was very easy to fall off the wagon when the station was next door to a Mexican restaurant.

He also wasn't able to count on one hand how many times he took people downstairs in a stair chair that couldn't walk, but an hour later he saw them skipping out of the hospital ER!

He was always the one to talk to the preschool classes as a probie, because all of the grown men he worked with are scared to death of public speaking in front of children for some reason.

It was also very common for confirmed "structure fires" to be false alarms!

Helping old ladies back into bed was actually pretty fufilling. Except the ones that had UTIs and started to fight you.

He found himself also not being able to sleep very well at home because he kept hearing phantom dispatch tones in his sleep.

As soon as he joined the fire department he had a sudden urge to golf in all of his spare time.

Which he didn't have a lot of because he had to get a second and third job because of the horrible pay.

But overall, Felix guessed it was worth finishing his
probation and getting to sit in a recliner.

Made in the USA
Las Vegas, NV
13 December 2024

14180299R00017

ISBN 9798300096083